The GINGERBREAD MAN LOOSE on the FIRE TRUCK

Laura Murray · illustrated by Mike Lowery

G. P. PUTNAM'S SONS · AN IMPRINT OF PENGUIN GROUP (USA) INC.

To my mom, Shirley, and my dad, Doug—
So much of who I am and what I strive to be
is a reflection of your love, encouragement, and guidance.
Thank you! With love, your youngest crumb-snatcher.

And a special thanks to the Fairfax County Fire and Rescue
Station # 1, McLean, Virginia—for your outstanding service
to our community, and your enthusiastic help
as I researched details of this book.
—L.M.

To my most favorit-est people
in the whole wide world:
Katrin and Allister.
—M.L.

G. P. PUTNAM'S SONS A division of Penguin Young Readers Group.
Published by The Penguin Group. Penguin Group (USA) Inc., 375 Hudson Street, New York, NY 10014,
U.S.A. Penguin Group (Canada), 90 Eglinton Avenue East, Suite 700, Toronto, Ontario M4P 2Y3, Canada
(a division of Pearson Penguin Canada Inc.). Penguin Books Ltd, 80 Strand, London WC2R 0RL, England.
Penguin Ireland, 25 St. Stephen's Green, Dublin 2, Ireland (a division of Penguin Books Ltd). Penguin
Group (Australia), 250 Camberwell Road, Camberwell, Victoria 3124, Australia (a division of Pearson
Australia Group Pty Ltd). Penguin Books India Pvt Ltd, 11 Community Centre, Panchsheel Park, New
Delhi - 110 017, India. Penguin Group (NZ), 67 Apollo Drive, Rosedale, Auckland 0632, New Zealand
(a division of Pearson New Zealand Ltd). Penguin Books South Africa, Rosebank Office Park, 181 Jan
Smuts Avenue, Parktown North 2193, South Africa. Penguin China, B7 Jiaming Center, 27 East Third
Ring Road North, Chaoyang District, Beijing 100020, China. Penguin Books Ltd, Registered Offices:
80 Strand, London WC2R 0RL, England.

Text copyright © 2013 by Laura Murray. Illustrations copyright © 2013 by Mike Lowery.
All rights reserved. No part of this book may be reproduced, scanned or distributed in any printed
or electronic form without permission in writing from the publisher, G. P. Putnam's Sons, a division of
Penguin Young Readers Group, 345 Hudson Street, New York, NY 10014. G. P. Putnam's Sons, Reg. U.S.
Pat & Tm. Off. Please do not participate in or encourage piracy of copyrighted materials in violation
of the author's rights. Purchase only authorized editions. The publisher does not have any control
over and does not assume any responsibility for author or third-party websites or their content.

Published simultaneously in Canada. Manufactured in China.
Design by Ryan Thomann. Text set in Bokka and Dr. Eric, with a bit of hand-lettering.
The illustrations were rendered with pencil, traditional screen printing, and digital color.

Library of Congress Cataloging-in-Publication Data
Murray, Laura, 1970- The Gingerbread Man loose on the fire truck / Laura Murray ; illustrated
by Mike Lowery. p. cm. Summary: When the Gingerbread Man joins the children who made him on a
school field trip to a fire station, he escapes being eaten by Spot the Dalmatian and rides along
to a fire. [1. Stories in rhyme. 2. Cookies—Fiction. 3. Fire departments—Fiction. 4. School field
trips—Fiction.] I. Lowery, Mike, 1980- ill. II. Title. PZ8.3.M9368Gjf 2013 [E]—dc23 2012029867
ISBN 978-0-399-25779-7
Special Markets ISBN 978-0-399-17668-5 Not for Resale
10 9 8 7 6 5 4 3

On a bright **Monday** morning, my teacher breezed in.

LET'S ALL MAKE A CIRCLE. IT'S TIME TO BEGIN.

FIRE TRUCK

She winked and then whispered,

OUR FIELD TRIP'S TODAY!

The pocket was cozy.
I peeked from the **top**.

The **bus** drove for miles,
then came to a **stop**.

In front of a building with shiny red **doors**
stood two **firefighters** from **Company Four**.

One had on **gear** for a quick **demonstration**,
and standing beside him was **Spot**, the **Dalmatian**.

HELMET

GOGGLES

OXYGEN
TANK

AXE

FLASH-
LIGHT

GLOVES

SPOT

BOOTS

I was **jostled** and **jiggled** as kids moved about.
Then I fell from the **pocket,**

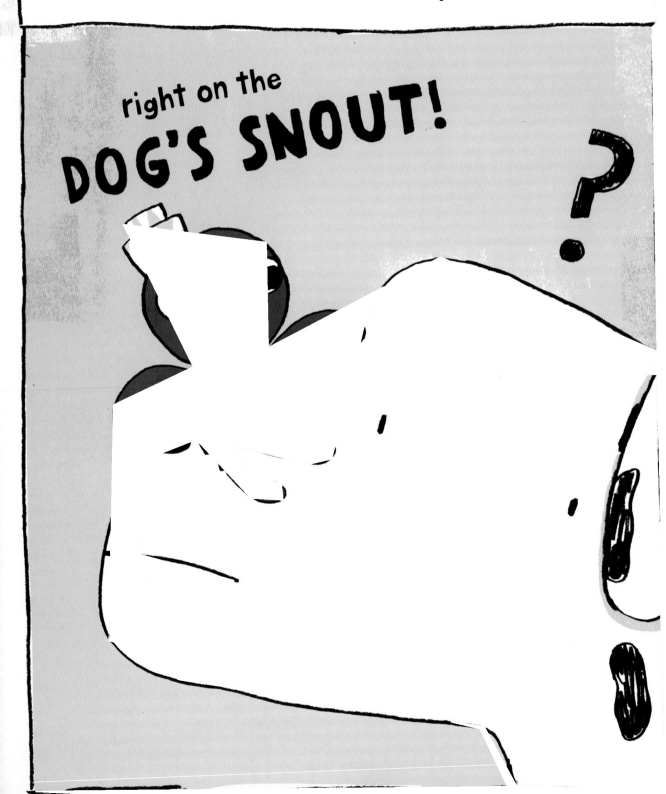

Spot **sniffed** at my face, taking one sticky **lick**.

I needed a **TRICK** to get out of there **QUICK!**

He **tossed** me up high with his mouth open **wide**,

but I **flipped** toward his tail and slid down, like a **slide**.

My feet hit the **ground**. I took off for the **station**,

but right on my **heels** was that hungry **Dalmatian**.

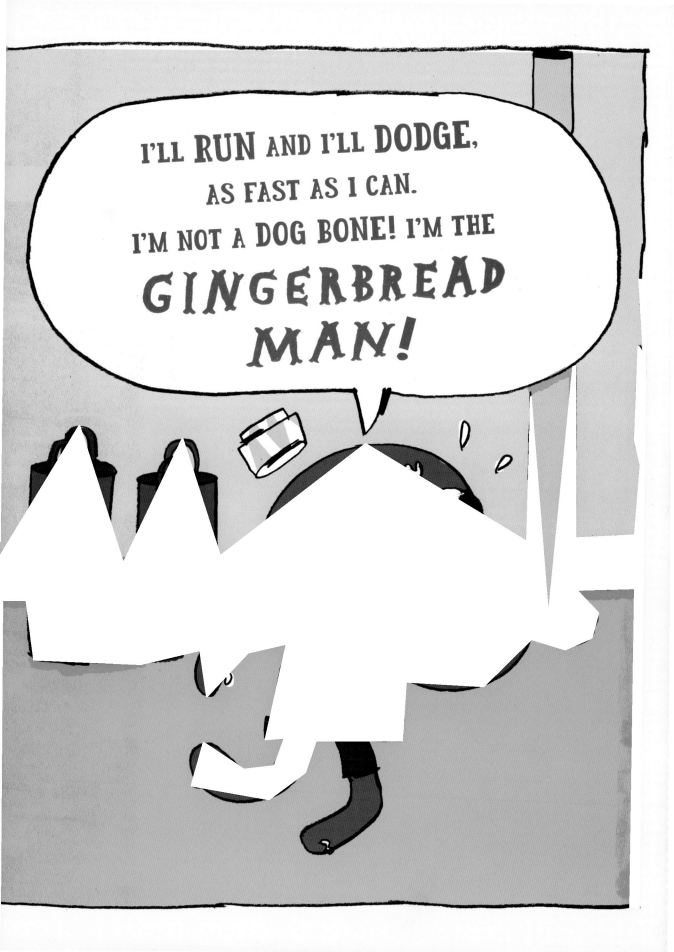

The class didn't notice. They tried on black **boots,**

and helmets, and air tanks, and big heavy suits.

I dashed to the fire truck,
jumped in a seat.

I **hopped** on the steering wheel, gave it a **spin**— and **yelled out**

HONK HONK!

with a big cookie **grin.**

The **wheel** spun past **gauges** and **switches** and **knobs**— and all kinds of **buttons** that do different **jobs.**

Then I heard someone **whistle**.
Spot trotted away,

So I **jumped** through the window
without a **delay**.

I landed on top of a big silver **bowl**.

OH NO!
I cried **out**
as I leapt for a **pole**.

SPOT

I shimmied
right up

and I **sprang** from the **top,** then jumped on a bed with a big **BELLY FLOP.**

There were several more bunks with their covers pulled **tight** for each **firefighter** who stayed through the **night.**

I **bounced** on each bed on my way to the **door,** then into a room with a bright checkered **floor.**

I peeked 'round the **corner** and smelled something **yummy**—

a grumbling sound **rumbled** up from my **tummy**.

SNIFF SNIFF

GRUMBLE

I spotted a fireman filling up bowls with **five-alarm chili** and buttery **rolls**.

Then all of a sudden, I heard a loud noise.

FIRE!

one shouted.

NO LUNCH FOR US, BOYS . . .

They rushed to the

UNK ROOM

and slid down the

POLE.

I followed behind them, then peered down the hole.

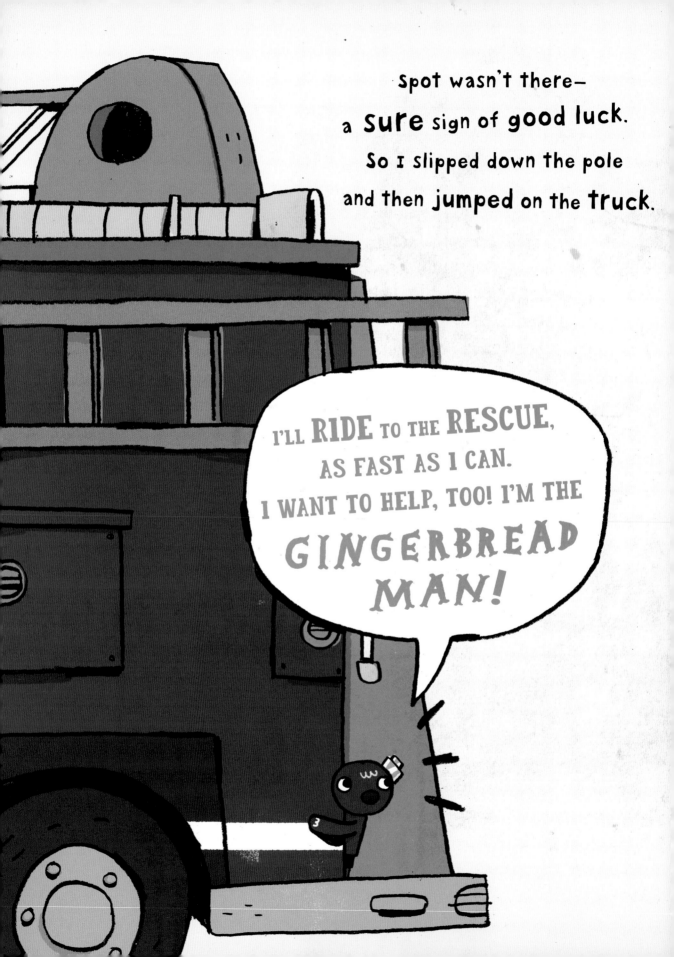

Spot wasn't there—
a **sure** sign of **good** luck.
So I slipped down the pole
and then **jumped** on the **truck**.

I'LL **RIDE** TO THE **RESCUE**,
AS FAST AS I CAN.
I WANT TO HELP, TOO! I'M THE
GINGERBREAD
MAN!

WHEEE-EEEEE

went the **SIRENS.** The lights flashed **around**

as I **zoomed** past my classmates, below on the **ground.**

we sped through the streets
and I clung to the **back**,

near **ladders** and **hoses**
piled up in a **stack**.

The engine pulled up. Firefighters jumped out.
They rushed to the hydrant and opened the spout.

I spied a large house with a shed near the back.
Smoke rose from its window, all sooty and black.

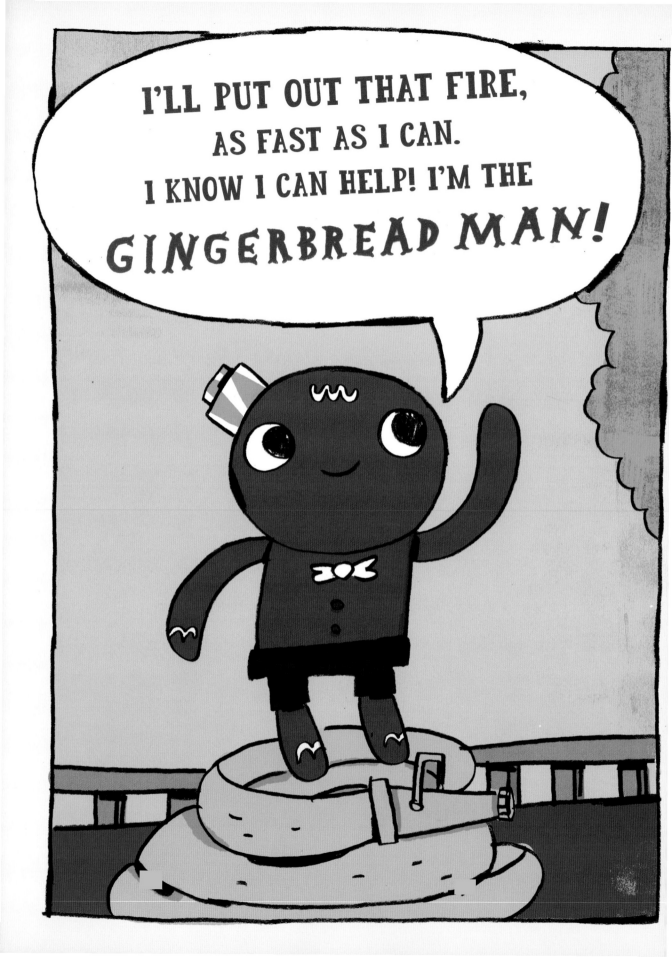

I grabbed the hose nozzle and gave it a **pull,**

but that hose whipped and bucked like a rodeo **bull.**

The water **whooshed** out and it doused the old **shed,** and the powerful spray shot the hat off my **head.**

The **chief** ran up **quickly** and dove on the **hose.**

She **crawled** her way up till we came **nose** to **nose.**

LOOK, EVERYONE!
IT'S A GINGERBREAD MAN.
NOW, WHERE DID YOU
COME FROM?

said Fire Chief Anne.

I CAME WITH THE CHILDREN
TO VISIT THE STATION.
BUT I ALMOST GOT EATEN BY
SPOT, THE DALMATIAN!

We packed up the **truck** and drove back to the **station**.
We pulled in the drive to a standing **ovation**.

The children **applauded** and shouted out "**YAY!**"
They held me up **high**, yelling,

YOU SAVED THE DAY!

YOU'RE REALLY A HERO!
YOU'RE PART OF OUR CREW,
BUT YOU'RE MISSING YOUR HAT,
SO WE HAVE ONE FOR YOU.

"A SHINY RED **HELMET**
FROM COMPANY FOUR!

THERE ARE MORE FOR
YOUR **CLASSMATES**
STACKED UP BY THE DOOR."

I tried on my helmet and shouted,

WOO-HOO! I'M A GINGERBREAD MAN AND A **FIREMAN**, TOO!